CW01642746

The Author

Ilse Cornwall Ross was born in Hamelin, Germany. She grew up in Germany but subsequently moved to Cambridge and decided to stay in England. Later, as a mature student, she took a degree in Literature and an MPhil. in History. She is a linguist, tutor and researcher with a particular interest in the nineteenth century. Her previous published works are the translation of an art book and the translation of a historical book on the German artist, Franz Klemmer. She has also edited two collections of poems. Ilse Cornwall Ross lives in Winchester.

Best wishes,

Ilse Cornwall Ross

23 September 1995

John Keats

A SEASON OF MELLOW FRUITFULNESS ~

JOHN KEATS
in
WINCHESTER
1819

by
ILSE CORNWALL ROSS

Illustrations by
JOAN MULLINS

ILEX TERRACE PRESS
WINCHESTER, HAMPSHIRE
1995

ILEX TERRACE PRESS
38, Romsey Road,
Winchester, Hampshire,
SO22 5DL

First Published1995

ISBN 0 9526333 0 2

Printed and bound in Great Britain by
Sarsen Press, Winchester, Hampshire.

Layout and Typeset by
P.F.Presentation, Winchester, Hampshire.

This book is dedicated with love to my children, Andrea, Renate, Verena and Gareth.

Acknowledgements

Grateful acknowledgement is made to the following for permission to reproduce copyright extracts:

Oxford University Press for letters and extracts from letters from *Letters of John Keats,* a selection edited by Robert Gittings, 1987

The London Borough of Camden (for biographical detail from the *Keats House Guide* and for reproduction of Keats's signature)

Manuscript of ode *To Autumn* by permission of the Houghton Library, Harvard University

I should also like to thank:

The Tourism Division of Winchester City Council for their support

Hampshire County Council Museums Service for permission to reproduce prints of Winchester

Hampshire Record Office for permission to reproduce a print of Winchester (page No 38) and a photo (page No. 52) from *Winchester Illustrated,* edited by William Thorn Warren, Warren & Son Ltd., 1913 (photo No. 27)

The British Library, London, for access to the Manuscript Room

Finally, I should like to express my gratitude to the following people who assisted me with information and encouragement:

Jehane Boden Spiers, Wendy Bowen, Sally Edwards, Patricia and Keith Flack, Mrs. Christina M. Gee, Matthew Huntley, Joan Mullins, Judy Simmons, Mrs. Philippa Stevens and the staff of the Local Studies section of Winchester Library, the staff of the Hampshire Record Office, the staff of the Winchester Cathedral Education Centre and my children, Andrea, Verena, Gareth and particularly, Renate, who shares Keats's belief with me that:

> A thing of beauty is a joy for ever:
> Its loveliness increases; it will never
> Pass into nothingness; but still will keep
> A bower quiet for us, and a sleep
> Full of sweet dreams, and health, and quiet breathing....
>
> (*Endymion*)

The great beauty of poetry is, that it makes every thing every place interesting - The palatine Venice and the abbotine Winchester are equally interesting.[1]

John Keats

Preface

John Keats (31st October 1795 - 23rd February 1821) has inspired many people through his writing and at the same time he has elicited much writing about himself. His poetry is studied and loved both here in England and abroad. I am delighted to have the opportunity in this small volume, to add my voice to the voices of scholars, interpreters and admirers of Keats. My intention is simple: I wish to set Keats in the context of the Winchester in which he lived, and his stay in Winchester in the context of his short life. In addition, I want to present to the reader the product of my imagination and my response to the material I found in my search for the background to the creation of one of the best known odes by John Keats - *To Autumn* - which was conceived and written in Winchester. I am also placing into context Kcats's fragment *King Stephen* and Part II of *Lamia*, both written in Winchester.

The primary sources for my research have been Keats's letters from Winchester. Keats himself points out the drawbacks of relying on letters for information:

> ....Writing has this disadvan[ta]ge of speaking. one cannot write a wink, or a nod, or a grin, or a purse of the Lips, or a *smile - O law!* One can-[not] put ones pinger [*for* finger] to one's nose, or yerk ye in the ribs, or lay hold of your button in writing - but in all the most lively and titterly parts of my Letter you must not fail to imagine me as the epic poets say - now here, now there, now with one foot pointed at the ceiling, now with another....[2]

However, his letters convey a vivid picture of his life and I do hope that *A Season of Mellow Fruitfulness* will have a small part to play in bringing Keats's important stay in Winchester to the attention of many people in this special year, in which we celebrate the 200th anniversary of his birth.

Winchester, September 1995

Ilse Cornwall Ross

I

Keats came to Winchester on 12th August 1819 from Shanklin on the Isle of Wight - ostensibly to find a library for background research in connection with the Play *Otho The Great* and poems on which he had been working. His permanent residence at that time was Wentworth Place in Hampstead.[3] However he had felt the need for a change to his lifestyle there. He had begun to register a feeling of being locked into money worries and a growing concern about a constant sore throat.[4] In addition, he was torn between his intense love for Fanny Brawne and his inability to consolidate that relationship. He also comments on feeling distracted from his writing through people calling and staying at Wentworth Place. Yet after about six weeks in Shanklin, he was beginning to realise the shortcomings of living there and he and his friend Charles Brown decided to travel to Winchester and take some cheap lodgings. He failed to locate a library in Winchester, but his letters seem to imply that instead he found something which would have been of much more consequence to his future life, had his health not deteriorated so quickly. As the story of his life in Winchester unfolds, we will come to discern what this was.

Keats stayed in Winchester for only two months.

However, to understand the significance of this relatively short time, we need to place it firmly in context. His life was to be a short one, even by the standard of his contemporaries. Life expectancy was around 42 years at the time: Keats lived for only 25 years and four months. His first chosen career had been that of an apothecary. On completing his training in 1816, he decided to devote his life to poetry. He was, at this stage, 21 years of age. But his time as an aspiring poet was to be cut tragically short. After October 1819 he did not write any significant poetry again. His literary career amounted to only three short years, of which scholars agree that the year 1819 was by far the most productive and formative. Two months of this year were spent in Winchester, during which time he worked intensely. For three weeks he lived entirely alone, deeply immersed in reading and writing. Set within the context of his life, the time Keats spent in Winchester has a significance that gives his writings of this period an entirely different poignancy and weight. For his time in Winchester inspired one of his best known poems, the ode *To Autumn*, a poem that has had a strong impact on scholars and general readers of poetry alike. It was in Winchester, too, that he began work on *King Stephen*, a drama steeped in this ancient city's heritage. Keats's letters from Winchester vividly set the poet in the place that so inspired him. A closer examination of the work he produced during his stay offers insights into the relationship between poet and place.

II

First, however, a brief look at Keats's life before coming to Winchester will serve to provide background to the information presented about his time here.[5]

Keats was born on 31st October 1895, probably at a livery stable and alehouse in Moorfields (now Moorgate), Finsbury, on the edge of London. He lost both his parents early in life. His father was killed by a fall from his horse, when Keats was only eight years old. His mother remarried shortly afterwards but she was not happy in her new marriage. She died when

Keats was only 14 years old. John Keats had two brothers: George (1797-1841) and Tom (1799-1818) and a sister, Frances Mary, known as Fanny (1803-1889). Their grandmother, Mrs Jennings, appointed two guardians and established a trust with a fund of £8,000.

Keats received a good education at the school of John Clarke in Enfield. Clarke's son, Charles Cowden Clarke, worked as a tutor at the school and he had a formative influence on John Keats. He introduced him to the study of literature and became a life-long friend. Keats's reading in the later years of his time at school included Burnet's *History of His Own Time*, Leigh Hunt's *Examiner,* Tooke's *Pantheon,* Mavor's *Collection* and *Universal History*, Robertson's Histories of Scotland, America, and Charles V, Lemprière's Dictionary, Tindal's abridgement of Spence's *Polymetis* and others.[6] After finishing school, Keats was apprenticed for five years to Mr. Hammond, a surgeon of repute at Edmonton. He transferred to Guy's and St. Thomas's hospitals, London, and qualified there as an apothecary in 1816, obtaining a licence of the Society of Apothecaries. As indicated earlier, it was then, at the age of 21, that he decided to immerse himself into the world of the imagination and become a poet.

Early in 1816, Charles Cowden Clarke had shown some of Keats's verses to the prominent critic and journalist, Leigh Hunt (1784-1859) in Hampstead. Hunt's reaction was favourable and he published

Keats's sonnet *To Solitude* in his paper *The Examiner* on 5th May 1816. Subsequently, Keats was associated with Leigh Hunt and his followers of radical repute, referred to by the critics as the 'Cockney School of Poetry'. Keats enjoyed meeting Hunt socially in Hampstead and he was introduced to poets, and artists of Hunt's circle, for instance the young poets Percy Bysshe Shelley (1792-1822), John Hamilton Reynolds (1794-1852), the painters, Benjamin Robert Haydon (1786-1846) and Joseph Severn (1793-1879). Hampstead was a village at this time and Keats found it very attractive. By the middle of April 1817, Keats and his brothers, George and Tom, had moved into lodgings in Well Walk, Hampstead.

The first volume of Keats's poetry was published in March 1817 by Ollier Brothers. This volume included sonnets and miscellaneous poems, amongst them *Sleep and Poetry.* The publication was a disappointment. The collection did not attract many buyers. However, another publisher became interested in Keats's talent: John Taylor (1781-1864) of Taylor and Hessey. He wrote to his father in April 1817: '*We have agreed for the next edition of Keats's poems. I cannot think he will fail to become a great poet.*'[7]

Amongst the people Keats met whilst living at Well Walk in Hampstead were Charles Wentworth Dilke, Charles Armitage Brown and Benjamin Bailey. When away from Hampstead, Keats kept in close contact with these friends through correspondence, as is evident from his letters written in Winchester.

The next publication, in April 1818, was Keats's poem *Endymion.* He had written *Endymion* and other poems in Teignmouth whilst looking after his younger brother, Tom, who had been sent there to alleviate the symptoms of tuberculosis. The poem was not kindly reviewed by the critics, because they continued to associate Keats with Leigh Hunt and his political radicalism.

Tom Keats died on 1st December 1818 and shortly afterwards Charles Brown asked John Keats whether he would like to move into Wentworth Place. Keats was grateful to do so. Here he was introduced to

Fanny Brawne, whose widowed mother had first temporarily moved into Wentworth Place and then permanently in April 1819. Keats felt immediately attracted to Fanny, and his feelings for her have found expression both in his many letters to her and in poems addressed to her. By the summer of 1819, shortly before Keats came to Winchester, they had come to an understanding about their future.

The spring and summer of the year 1819 was a very productive period for Keats. Five of the six great Odes were written in the spring: *To Psyche*, *On Indolence*, *On Melancholy*, *To a Nightingale*, *On a Grecian Urn*. Furthermore, he started *Lamia*, wrote *La Belle Dame Sans Merci* and sonnets. We owe it to Charles Brown, who made copies of Keats's letters, and to another friend of Keats, Richard Woodhouse (1788-1834), reader to Taylor and Hessey, that so much of Keats's writing has been preserved.

III

In order to have a change of environment, Keats and Brown travelled to Shanklin on the Isle of Wight at the end of June 1819. From here, Keats wrote passionate love letters to Fanny, which are beautiful and expressive:

> My sweet Girl,
> Your Letter gave me more delight, than any thing in the world but yourself could do; indeed I am almost astonished that any absent one should have that luxurious power over my senses which I feel. Even when I am not thinking of you I receive your

influence and a tenderer nature steeling upon me. All my thoughts, my unhappiest days and nights have I find not at all cured me of my love of Beauty, but made it so intense that I am miserable that you are not with me: or rather breathe in that dull sort of patience that cannot be called Life. I never knew before, what such a love as you have made me feel, was; I did not believe in it; my Fancy was affraid of it, lest it should burn me up. But if you will fully love me, though there may be some fire, 't will not be more than we can bear when moistened and bedewed with Pleasures. You mention 'horrid people' and ask me whether it depend upon them, whether I see you again - Do understand me, my love, in this - I have so much of you in my heart that I must turn Mentor when I see a chance of ha[r]m beffaling you. I would never see any thing but Pleasure in your eyes, love on your lips, and Happiness in your steps. I would wish to see you among those amusements suitable to your inclinations and spirits; so that our loves might be a delight in the midst of Pleasures agreeable enough, rather than a resource from vexations and cares - But I doubt much, in case of the worst, whether I shall be philosopher enough to follow my own Lessons: if I saw my resolution give you a pain I could not. Why may I not speak of your Beauty, since without that I could never have lov'd you - I cannot conceive any beginning of such love as I have for you but Beauty. There may be a sort of love for which, without the least sneer at it, I have the highest respect, and can admire it in others: but it has not the richness, the bloom, the full form, the enchantment of love after my own heart. So let me speak of you Beauty, though to my own endangering; if you could be so cruel to me as to try elsewhere its Power. You say you are affraid I shall think you do not love me - in saying this you make me ache the more to be near you. I am at the diligent use of my faculties here, I do not pass a day without sprawling some blank verse or tagging some rhymes; and here I must confess, that, (since I am on that subject,) I love you the more in that I believe you have liked me for my own sake and for nothing else - I have met with women whom I really think would like to be married to a Poem and to be given away by a Novel. I have seen your Comet, and only wish it was a sign that poor Rice would get well whose illness makes him rather a melancholy companion: and the more so as so to conquer his feelings and hide them from me, with a forc'd Pun. I kiss'd your writing over in the hope you had indulg'd me by leaving a trace of honey - What was your dream? Tell it me and I will tell you the interpretation thereof.

Ever yours my love!

John Keats -

Do not accuse me of delay - we have not here an opportunity of sending letters every day - Write speedily - [8]

My love,

I have been in so irritable a state of health these two or three last days, that I did not think I should be able to write this week. Not that I was so ill, but so much so as only to be capable of an unhealthy teasing letter. To night I am greatly recovered only to feel the languor I have felt after you touched with ardency. You say you perhaps might have made me better: you would then have made me worse: now you could quite effect a cure: What fee my sweet Physician would I not give you to do so. Do not call it folly, when I tell you I took your letter last night to bed with me. In the morning I found your name on the sealing wax obliterated. I was startled at the bad omen till I recollected that it must have happened in my dreams, and they you know fall out by contraries. You must have found out by this time I am a little given to bode ill like the raven; it is my misfortune not my fault; it has proceeded from the general tenor of the circumstances of my life, and rendered every event suspicious. However I will no more trouble either you or myself with sad Prophecies; though so far I am pleased at it as it has given me opportunity to love your disinterestedness towards me. I can be a raven no more; you and pleasure take possession of me at the same moment....I have been, I cannot tell why, in capital spirits this last hour. What reason? When I have to take my candle and retire to a lonely room, without the thought as I fall asleep, of seeing you tomorrow morning? or the next day, or the next - it takes on the appearance of impossibility and eternity - I will say a month - I will say I will see you in a month at most, though no one but yourself should see me; if it be but for an hour. I should not like to be so near you as London without being continually with you: after having once more kissed you Sweet I would rather be here alone at my task than in the bustle and hateful literary chit-chat. Meantime you must write to me - as I will every week - for your letters keep me alive. My sweet Girl I cannot speak my love for you. Good night! and

Ever yours

John Keats[9]

Fanny Brawne

My sweet Girl,

I hope you did not blame me much for not obeying your request of a Letter on Saturday: we have had four in our small room playing at cards night and morning leaving me no undisturb'd opportunity to write. Now Rice and Martin are gone, I am at liberty. Brown to my sorrow confirms the account you give of your ill health. You cannot conceive how I ache to be with you: how I would die for one hour - for what is in the world? I say you cannot conceive; it is impossible you should look with such eyes upon me as I have upon you: it cannot be. Forgive me if I wander a little this evening, for I have been all day employ'd in a very abstr[a]ct Poem and I am in deep love with you - two things which must excuse me. I have, believe me, not been an age in letting you take possession of me; the very first week I knew you I wrote myself your vassal; but burnt the Letter as the very next time I saw you I thought you manifested some dislike to me. If you should ever feel for Man at the first sight what I did for you, I am lost. Yet I should not quarrel with you, but hate myself if such a thing were to happen - only I should burst if the thing were not as fine as a Man as you are as a Woman. Perhaps I am too vehement, then fancy me on my knees, especially when I mention a part of you Letter which hurt me; you say speaking of Mr. Severn "but you must be satisfied in knowing that I admired you much more than your friend." My dear love, I cannot believe there ever was or ever could be any thing to admire in me especially as far as sight goes - I cannot be admired, I am not a thing to be admired. You are, I love you; all I can bring you is a swooning admiration of your Beauty. I hold that place among Men which snub-nos'd brunettes with meeting eyebrows do among women - they are trash to me - unless I should find one among them with a fire in her heart like the one that burns in mine. You absorb me in spite of myself - you alone: for I look not forward with any pleasure to what is call'd being settled in the world; I tremble at domestic cares - yet for you I would meet them, though if it would leave you the happier I would rather die than do so. I have two luxuries to brood over in my walks, your Loveliness and the hour of my death. O that I could have possession of them both in the same minute. I hate the world: it batters too much the wings of my self-will, and would I could take a sweet poison from your lips to send me out of it. From no others would I take it. I am indeed astonish'd to find myself so careless of all cha[r]ms but yours - remembring as I do the time when even a bit of ribband was a matter of interest with me. What softer words can I find for you after this - what it is I will not read. Nor will I say more here, but in a Postscript answer any thing else you may have mentioned in your letter in so many words - for I am distracted with a thousand thoughts. I will imagine you Venus to night and pray, pray, pray to your star like a Hethen.

Your's ever, fair Star,
John Keats[10]

Whilst in Shanklin, Keats worked with Brown on writing *Otho The Great,* a drama they hoped would be performed at Drury Lane and star the famous actor, Edmund Kean. Brown provided the plot and Keats then wrote the dramatic text.

By now the constant sore throat from which Keats had been suffering for some time was causing him increasing concern. He had, after all, only fairly recently experienced his brother's death from consumption. Financial worries were also building up which are later reflected in some of his letters from Winchester. Away from the comfort and company of his group of friends in Hampstead and, more particularly, separated from his beloved Fanny, his various frustrations suddenly became projected on to the place in which he was:

> ....I long to be off for Winchester for I begin to dislike the very door posts[s] here - the names, the pebbles....I was alone for a couple of days while Brown went gadding over the country with his ancient knapsack. Now I like his society as wells (*for* well) as any Man's, yet regretted his return - it broke in upon me like a Thunderbolt - I had got in a dream among my Books - really luxuriating in a solitude and silence you alone should have disturb'd - [11]

Keats and Brown decided to travel on to Winchester to find a library but it can be assumed that other considerations might also have played a part. Keats could not contemplate marrying Fanny without being able to offer her some degree of financial stability. This he hoped to provide by his writing, but the reception he had received so far by the critics had been devastating. His latest hope was to make an impact through the play *Otho the Great* but it required background research. Absence from Fanny made him love her all the more. He started to experience pangs of jealousy at the thought that she was able to enjoy a lively social life without him. However, what must have troubled him most was that he had noticed the first signs of having contracted tuberculosis.

He had set himself the task of achieving a breakthrough in his writing. Winchester would provide access to books, it had been the capital of ancient England, and must therefore have a lot to offer. Transport to London by coach would be considerably easier - being on the direct route from Southampton to London - and the postal service would be quicker. He was looking forward to receiving Fanny's letters and reading them in

Winchester Cathedral - walking up and down the aisles.[12] Finally, a change of climate might do him good. It is interesting to note that although he was longing to be with Fanny, Keats did not return to Hampstead at this stage. He remained in his world of books and writing and continued with his ambition to make his mark on the literary world by transferring to another solitary place, rented accommodation in the centre of Winchester, shared with Brown for some of the stay.

IV

Keats belonged to the Romantic movement - a movement that emphasised sincerity, spontaneity and originality. For the Romantics, a passionate insistence on the individual's freedom of expression marked a shift away from prescribed forms and accepted truths. By presenting the following excerpts from his Winchester letters and supplying prints of Winchester, mostly from the period of his stay, my aim is to engender in the reader a reaction akin to the Romantic movement.

> We removed to Winchester for the convenience of a Library and find it an exceeding pleasant Town, enriched with a beautiful Cathedrall and surrounded by a fresh-looking country. We are in tolerably good and cheap Lodgings. Within these two Months I have written 1500 Lines, most of which besides many more of prior composition you will probably see by next Winter. I have written two Tales, one from Boccacio call'd the Pot of Basil; and another call'd St Agnes' Eve on a popular superstition; and a third call'd Lamia - (half finished - I [hav]e a[l]so been writing parts of my Hyperion and [c]ompleted 4 Acts of a Tragedy It was the opinion of most of my friends that I should never be

Winchester from St. Giles's Hill

able to [write] a [s]cene - I will endeavour to wipe awa[y the prejudice -] I sincerely hope you will be pleased when my Labours since we last saw each other shall reach you - One of my Ambitions is tomake as great a revolution in modern dramatic writing as Kean has done in acting - another to upset the drawling of the blue stocking literary world - if in the course of a few years I do these two things I ought to die content ....[13]

....This Winchester is a fine place; a beautiful Cathedral and many other ancient building[s] in the Environs....[14]

....However we like it very much: it is the pleasantest Town I ever was in, and has the most reccommendations of any. There is a fine Cathedrall which to me is always a sourse of amusement; part of it built 1400 years ago; and the more modern by a magnificant Man, you may have read of in our History, called William of Wickham. The whole town is beautifully wooded - From the Hill at the eastern extremity you see a prospect of Streets, and old Buildings mixed up with Trees - Then There are the most beautiful streams about I ever saw - full of Trout - There is the Foundation of St. Croix about half a mile in the fields - a charity greatly abused - We have a Collegiate School, a

Winchester from the North East

roman catholic School; a chapel ditto and a Nunnery! And what improves it all is, the fashionable inhabitants are all gone to Southampton....[15]

....Since I have been at Winchester I have been improving in health - it is not so confined - and there is on one side of the city a dry chalky down where the air is worth six pence a pint....[16]

....The side streets here are excessively maiden-lady like: the door steps always fresh from the flannel. The knockers have a staid serious, nay almost awful quietness about them. - I never saw so quiet a collection of Lions' & Rams' heads - The doors most part black, with a little brass handle just above the keyhole, so that in Winchester a man may very quietly shut himself out of his own house....[17]

....This Winchester is a place tolerably well suited to me; there is a fine Cathedral, a College, A Roman-Catholic Chapel, a Methodist do, an independent do, - and there is not one loom or any thing like manufacturing beyond bread & butter in the whole City. ...It is a respectable, ancient aristocratical place... [18]

....The High Street is as quiet as a Lamb; the knockers are dieted To three raps per diem. The walks about are interresting - from the many old Buildings and arch ways -

The view of the high street through the Gate of the City, in the beautiful September evening light has amused me frequently....[19]

In comparison, a cursory glance at the copies of the Hampshire Chronicle and Courtier - South and West of England Pilot (as the present Hampshire Chronicle was then called), shows that Winchester at that time was an active market town - there are references to trading prices and the corn exchange in every issue.

National political reports and reports on court proceedings also play a prominent part, as well as local news, of course. As Keats arrived on 12th August, he just missed a great annual fair on Magdalen Hill, where large amounts of cheese were 'pitched'. On 16th August he may or may not have taken part in the Annual Melon Feast at the Globe Inn. On 14th August, the Prince Regent was in Southampton, and on 4th October it was the day for the new Mayor to commence office. The ceremony of swearing in took place at St. Michael's Church, followed by an elegant dinner at Dolphins.[20] Keats actually mentions seeing the yacht of the Prince Regent in Southampton in his letter of 16th August to Fanny Brawne and also the election of the new mayor in a letter to Reynolds of 21st September 1819.

Keats was pleased with his room and the view from it on to a blank wall in contrast to the sea view in Shanklin. This preference for a blank wall may well indicate that he wanted to be free from any other stimulation to his senses. This assumption is confirmed by his statement in a letter to Fanny Brawne: 'My Mind is heap'd to the full; stuff'd like a cricket ball - if I strive to fill it more it would burst.'[21] The impression from his letters is that he wished to be single-minded and able to give his full concentration to his writing.

Keats's Walk

There has been speculation about where exactly Keats lived in Winchester. He describes a daily walk which gives certain indications. At the start of this description he states:

> ....Now the time is beautiful. I take a walk every day for an hour before dinner and this is generally my walk - I go out at the back gate across one street, into the Cathedral yard, which is always interesting....
>
> ....then I pass under the trees along a paved path.... pass the beautiful front of the Cathedral....,

Winchester Cathedral, North East View

Winchester Cathedral, North West View

Winchester Cathedral, The Nave Looking East

Winchester Cathedral, The North Transept

....turn to the left under a stone door way - then I am on the other side of the building - which leaving behind me I pass on through two college-like squares seemingly built for the dwelling place of Deans and Prebendaries - garnished with grass and shaded with trees....,

...Then I pass through one of the old city gates....,

....and then you are in one College-Street through which I pass....

St. Mary's College, now Winchester College

St. Mary's College, now Winchester College

.... and at the end thereof crossing some meadows and at last a country alley of gardens...',

Winchester, Water Meadows

Winchester, Water Meadows

....I arrive, that is, my worship arrives at the foundation of Saint Cross, which is a very interesting old place, both for its gothic tower and alms-square and for the appropriation of its rich rents to ~~the~~ a relation of the Bishop of Winchester ....,

The Hospital of St. Cross

St Cross, North East View

Church of St. Cross, Interior

....Then I pass across St Cross meadows till you come to the most beautifully clear river - now this is only one mile of my walk I will spare you the other two till after supper when they would do you more good - You must avoid going the first mile just after dinner....[22] (Dinner at the time of Keats's stay was at approximately 3 p.m.)[23]

Looking at a number of street maps and particularly at the following one, we can assume that he must have lived in the western part of Colebrook Street, which then ran parallel to Paternoster Row.[24]

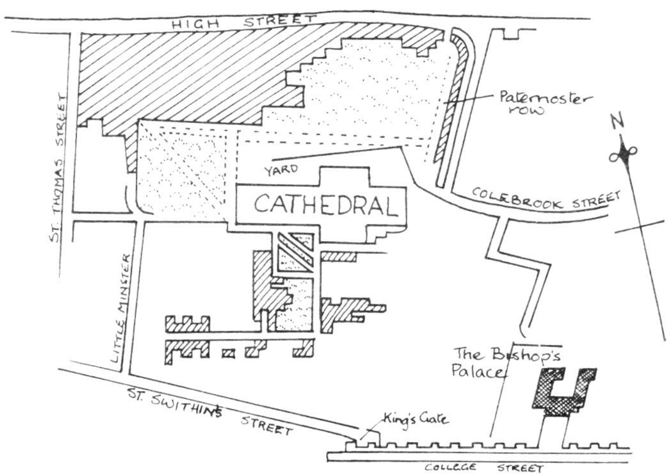

The following photo gives an impression of Paternoster Row, with a view on to the cathedral. On the right, an entrance can be discerned as well as the lime trees under which Keats walked.[25]

On his walk Keats thus experienced the majestic buildings of the cathedral, walked through the ancient Kingsgate, then along College Street. First he passed ROBBINS bookshop - now WELLS bookshop

- possibly browsing in there or even purchasing books. Then he passed the house in which Jane Austen had died only two years earlier. There does not seem to be any evidence that he was aware of Jane Austen's time in Winchester.

After this, he walked past the gate of St. Mary's College, now Winchester College. The term started around 1st September at the time, [26] and he would have encountered masters and boys to-ing and fro-ing, and may possibly have been reminded of his own school days and his friend Cowden Clarke.

Finally, turning into the Water Meadows, he was able to commune with nature, observing the wild-life on the river and the trees and plants in the changing autumnal season. Keats would then have reached the Foundation of St. Cross, possibly entering it, as he observed that there was 'an interesting Picture of Albert Durer's in there'.[27]

Then he would have walked a little further beyond the church of St. Cross, on a path to the left of it until he came to the 'chalky down where the air is worth 6d a pint' of his earlier description.

We do not know how he returned to his lodgings. At Keats's time there was a publication available which described some walks in Winchester in detail. The walk to St. Cross church would have taken him through Kingsgate and along Kingsgate Street, St. Faith's Road and Back Street.[28]

On his return to his lodgings for dinner, Keats may well have heard the sounds of evensong from the Cathedral. This was held at 3 p.m. at the time. Evensong was sung without the support of the organ in the autumn of 1819, as the organ was temporarily dismantled. It is possible that services were held in the Lady Chapel.[29]

V

Once established in his lodgings, Keats started a disciplined routine of reading and writing, interspersed by his daily walk. His first priority was to complete *Otho the Great,* the final act of which he wrote by himself, without being given the plot by Brown. The intention was not only to improve his financial situation through a successful play but he also planned to revolutionise drama and create a major rôle for his favourite actor, Edmund Kean, whom he had seen in the rôle of Richard III at Drury Lane.[30] According to Brown,[31] Keats started a new play, *King Stephen*, immediately after he had completed *Otho the Great*. The idea of writing a play about King Stephen was suggested to Keats by Brown. There is no doubt that inspiration for this play must have come from an awareness of the importance of King Stephen in the history of Winchester, where the Round Table hung on the eastern wall of the Great Hall at the time of Keats's stay in Winchester (it was moved to the western wall in 1874).[32] The historical background and the events during King Stephen's reign would have made excellent drama and provided a powerful part for Kean whom Keats adored. He felt that the rôle of King Stephen would be a more suitable one for Kean than the rôle of Ludolph in *Otho the Great*. Keats wrote the first 130 lines very quickly, probably for two reasons: he had recently had considerable experience in writing drama; and there was no shortage of background material for *King Stephen* in Winchester.

King Stephen

A brief glance at the history of King Stephen (1135-1154) makes clear the suitability for a historical drama of Shakespearean proportions: Stephen was the son of William the Conqueror's daughter, Adela. Favoured by his uncle, Henry I, he was crowned King after Henry's death, despite the fact that he had previously given support to Henry's daughter, Matilda, as heir to the throne. Matilda was unable to accept Stephen's accession to the throne and in 1139 she established an alternative court. This was the cause of civil war throughout much of Stephen's reign. At one stage Stephen was captured at Lincoln but was rescued by his Queen, also called Matilda. Finally, peace was achieved in 1153 through the Treaty of Westminster. Stephen accepted Matilda's son,

Henry, as his adopted son and heir. His elder son, Eustace, died before him and his other son, William, did not wish to be King. Stephen died in 1154 and was buried at Faversham.

The fragment *King Stephen* is certainly worth examining. It indicates that Keats might well have succeeded in making a breakthrough into writing successfully for the stage.

However, around the 16th August his hopes were crushed.[33] He read in a journal that Kean was going to America, so that even *Otho the Great*, if accepted, was not going to be performed until the following year. This was too late; Keats needed a breakthrough now.

He immediately changed his tactics, dropped the play, and reverted to writing poetry with the intention of completing a volume of poems for publication. His first objective was to finish *Lamia*, the first part of which he had written in Shanklin. He wrote Part II of *Lamia* in the last week of August and the first days of September, 1819, at his usual rate of about thirty lines a day.[34]

Love in a hut, with water and a crust,
Is - Love, forgive us ! - cinders, ashes, dust;
Love in a palace is perhaps at last
More grievous torment than a hermit's fast:
That is a doubtful tale from faery land,
Hard for the non-elect to understand.
Had Lucius lived to hand his story down,
He might have given the moral a fresh frown,
Or clenched it quite: but too short was their bliss
To breed distrust and hate, that make the soft voice hiss.
Besides, there, nightly, with terrific glare,
Love, jealous grown at so complete a pair,
Hovered and buzzed his wings, with fearful roar,
Above the lintel of their chamber door,
And down the passage cast a glow upon the floor.

For all this came a ruin: side by side
They were enthroned, in the even-tide,
Upon a couch, near to a curtaining
Whose airy texture, from a golden string,
Floated into the room, and let appear
Unveiled the summer heaven, blue and clear,
Betwixt two marble shafts:- there they reposed,
Where use had made it sweet, with eyelids closed,
Saving a tithe which love still open kept,
That they might see each other while they almost slept;
When from the slope side of a suburb hill,

Deafening the swallow's twitter, came a thrill
Of trumpets - Lycius started - the sounds fled,
But left a thought, a buzzing in his head.
For the first time, since first he harbouring in
The purple-lined palace of sweet sin,
His spirit passed beyond its golden bourn
Into the noisy world almost foresworn.
The lady, ever watchful, penetrant,
Saw this with pain, so arguing a want
Of something more, more than her empery
Of joys; and she began to moan and sigh
Because he mused beyond her, knowing well
That but a moment's thought is passion's passing bell.
"Why do you sigh, fair creature?" whispered he.
"Why do you think?" returned she, tenderly:
"You have deserted me;- where am I now?
Not in your heart while care weighs on your brow:
No, no, you have dismissed me; and I go
From your breast houseless: ay, it must be so."
He answered, bending to her open eyes,
Where he was mirrored small in paradise:
"My silver planet, both of eve and morn!
Why will you plead yourself so sad forlorn,
While I am striving how to fill my heart
With deeper crimson, and a double smart?
How to entangle, trammel up and snare
Your soul in mine, and labyrinth you there
Like the hid scent in an unbudded rose?

Ay, a sweet kiss - you see your mighty woes.
My thoughts! shall I unveil them? Listen then!
What mortal hath a prize, that other men
May be confounded and abashed withal,
But lets it sometimes pace abroad majestical,
And triumph, as in thee I should rejoice
Amid the hoarse alarm of Corinth's voice.
Let my foes choke, and my friends shout afar,
While through the thronged streets your bridal car
Wheels round its dazzling spokes." - The lady's cheek
Trembled; she nothing said, but, pale and meek,
Arose and knelt before him, wept a rain
Of sorrows at his words; at last with pain
Beseeching him, the while his hand she wrung,
To change his purpose. He thereat was stung,
Perverse, with stronger fancy to reclaim
Her wild and timid nature to his aim:
Besides, for all his love, in self-despite,
Against his better self, he took delight
Luxurious in her sorrows, soft and new.
His passion, cruel grown, took on a hue
Fierce and sanguineous as 'twas possible
In one whose brow had no dark veins to swell.
Fine was the mitigated fury, like
Apollo's presence when in act to strike
The serpent - Ha, the serpent! certes, she
Was none. She burnt, she loved the tyranny,
And, all subdued, consented to the hour

When to the bridal he should lead his paramour.
Whispering in midnight silence, said the youth,
"Sure some sweet name thou hast, though, by my truth,
I have not asked it, ever thinking thee
Not mortal, but of heavenly progeny,
As still I do. Hast any mortal name,
Fit appellation for this dazzling frame?
Or friends or kinsfolk on the citied earth,
To share our marriage feast and nuptial mirth?"
"I have no friends," said Lamia, "no, not one;
My presence in wide Corinth hardly known:
My parents' bones are in their dusty urns
Sepulchred, where no kindled incense burns,
Seeing all their luckless race are dead, save me,
And I neglect the holy rite for thee.
Even as you list invite your many guests;
But if, as now it seems, your vision rests
With any pleasure on me, do not bid
Old Appollonius - from him keep me hid."
Lycius, perplexed at words so blind and blank,
Made close inquiry; from whose touch she shrank,
Feigning a sleep; and he to the dull shade
Of deep sleep in a moment was betrayed.

It was the custom then to bring away
The bride from home at blushing shut of day,
Veiled, in a chariot, heralded along
By strewn flowers, torches, and a marriage song,

With other pageants: but this fair unknown
Had not a friend. So being left alone
(Lycius was gone to summon all his kin),
And knowing surely she could never win
His foolish heart from its mad pompousness,
She set herself, high-thoughted, how to dress
The misery in fit magnificence.
She did so, but 'tis doubtful how and whence
Came, and who were her subtle servitors.
About the halls, and to and from the doors,
There was a noise of wings, till in short space
The glowing banquet-room shone with wide-arched grace.
A haunting music, sole perhaps and lone
Supportress of the faery-roof, made moan
Throughout, as fearful the whole charm might fade.
Fresh carved cedar, mimicking a glade
Of palm and plantain, met from either side,
High in the midst, in honour of the bride:
Two palms and then two plantains, and so on,
From either side their stems branched one to one
All down the aisled place; and beneath all
There ran a stream of lamps straight on from wall to wall.
So canopied, lay an untasted feast
Teeming with odours. Lamia, regal drest,
Silently paced about, and as she went,
In pale contented sort of discontent,
Missioned her viewless servants to enrich
The fretted splendour of each nook and niche.

Between the tree-stems, marbled plain at first,
Came jasper panels; then, anon, there burst
Forth creeping imagery of slighter trees,
And with the larger wove in small intricacies.
Approving all, she faded at self-will,
And shut the chamber up, close, hushed and still,
Complete and ready for the revels rude,
When dreadful guests would come to spoil her solitude.

The day appeared, and all the gossip rout.
O senseless Lycius! Madman! wherefore flout
The silent-blessing fate, warm and cloistered hours,
And show to common eyes these secret bowers?
The herd approached; each guest, with busy brain,
Arriving at the portal, gazed amain,
And entered marvelling: for they knew the street,
Remembered it from childhood all complete
Without a gap, yet ne'er before had seen
That royal porch, that high-built fair demesne;
So in they hurried all, mazed, curious and keen:
Save one, who looked thereon with eye severe,
And with calm-planted steps walked in austere:
'Twas Apollonius: something too he laughed,
As though some knotty problem, that had daft
His patient thought, had now begun to thaw,
And solve and melt: 'twas just as he foresaw.

He met within the murmurous vestibule

His young disciple. "'Tis no common rule,
Lycius," said he, "for uninvited guest
To force himself upon you, and invest
With an unbidden presence the bright throng
Of younger friends; yet must I do this wrong,
And you forgive me." Lycius blushed, and led
The old man through the inner doors broad-spread;
With reconciling words and courteous mien
Turning into sweet milk the sophist's spleen.

Of wealthy lustre was the banquet-room,
Filled with pervading brilliance and perfume:
Before each lucid panel fuming stood
A censer fed with myrrh and spiced wood,
Each by a secret tripod held aloft,
Whose slender feet wide-swerved upon the soft
Wool-woofed carpets: fifty wreaths of smoke
From fifty censers their light voyage took
To the high roof, still mimicked as they rose
Along the mirrored walls by twin-clouds odorous.
Twelve sphered tables, by silk seats insphered,
High as the level of a man's breast reared
On libbard's paws, upheld the heavy gold
Of cups and goblets, and the store thrice told
Of Ceres' horn, and, in huge vessels, wine
Came from the gloomy tun with merry shine.
Thus loaded with a feast the tables stood,
Each shrining in the midst the image of a God.

When in the antechamber every guest
Had felt the cold full sponge to pleasure pressed,
By minist'ring slaves, upon his hands and feet,
And fragrant oils with ceremony meet
Poured on his hair, they all moved to the feast
In white robes, and themselves in order placed
Around the silken couches, wondering
Whence all this mighty cost and blaze of wealth could spring.

Soft went the music the soft air along,
While fluent Greek and vowelled undersong
Kept up among the guests, discoursing low
At first, for scarcely was the wine at flow;
But when the happy vintage touched their brains,
Louder they talk, and louder come the strains
Of powerful instruments:- the gorgeous dyes,
The space, the splendour of the draperies,
The roof of awful richness, nectarous cheer,
Beautiful slaves, and Lamia's self, appear,
Now, when the wine has done its rosy deed,
And every soul from human trammels freed,
No more so strange; for merry wine, sweet wine,
Will make Elysian shades not too fair, too divine.
Soon was God Bacchus at meridian height;
Flushed were their cheeks, and bright eyes double bright:
Garlands of every green, and every scent
From vales deflowered, or forest-trees branch-rent,

In baskets of bright osiered gold were brought
High as the handles heaped, to suit the thought
Of every guest; that each, as he did please,
Mighty fancy-fit his brows, silk-pillowed at his ease.

What wreath for Lamia? What for Lycius?
What for the sage, old Apollonius?
Upon her aching forehead be there hung
The leaves of willow and of adder's tongue,
And for the youth, quick, let us strip for him
The thyrsus, that his watching eyes may swim
Into forgetfulness; and for the sage,
Let spear-grass and the spiteful thistle wage
War on his temples. Do not all charms fly
At the mere touch of cold philosophy?
There was an awful rainbow once in heaven:
We know her woof, her texture; she is given
In the dull catalogue of common things.
Philosophy will clip an angel's wings,
Conquer all mysteries by rule and line,
Empty the haunted air, and gnomed mine-
Unweave a rainbow, as it erewhile made
The tender-personed Lamia melt into a shade.

By her glad Lycius sitting, in chief place,
Scarce saw in all the room another face,
Till, checking his love trance, a cup he took
Full brimmed, and opposite sent forth a look

'Cross the broad table, to beseech a glance
From his old teacher's wrinkled countenance,
And pledge him. The bald-head philosopher
Had fixed his eye, without a twinkle or stir,
Full on the alarmed beauty of the bride,
Brow-beating her fair form, and troubling her sweet pride.
Lycius then pressed her hand, with devout touch,
As pale it lay upon the rosy couch:
Twas icy, and the cold ran through his veins;
Then sudden it grew hot, and all the pains
Of an unnatural heat shot to his heart.
"Lamia, what means this? Wherefore dost thou start?
Know'st thou that man?" Poor Lamia answered not.
He gazed into her eyes, and not a jot
Owned they the love-lorn piteous appeal:
More, more he gazed: his human senses reel:
Some hungry spell that loveliness absorbs;
There was no recognition in those orbs.
"Lamia!" he cried - and no soft-toned reply.
The many heard, and the loud revelry
Grew hush; the stately music no more breathes;
The myrtle sickened in a thousand wreaths.
By faint degrees, voice, lute, and pleasure ceased;
A deadly silence step by step increased,
Until it seemed a horrid presence there,
And not a man but felt a terror in his hair.
"Lamia!" he shrieked; and nothing but the shriek
With its sad echo did the silence break.

"Begone, foul dream!" he cried, gazing again
In the bride's face, where now no azure vein
Wandered on fair-spaced temples; no soft bloom
Misted the cheek; no passion to illume
The deep-recessed vision:-all was blight;
Lamia, no longer fair, there sat a deadly white.
"Shut, shut those juggling eyes, thou ruthless man!
Turn them aside, wretch! or the righteous ban
Of all the Gods, whose dreadful images
Here represent their shadowy presences,
May pierce them on the sudden with the thorn
Of painful blindness; leaving thee forlorn,
In trembling dotage to the feeblest fright
Of conscience, for their long offended might,
For all thine impious proud-heart sophistries,
Unlawful magic, and enticing lies.
Corinthians! look upon that grey-beard wretch!
Mark how, posessed, his lashless eyelids stretch
Around his demon eyes! Corinthians, see!
My sweet bride withers at their potency."
"Fool!" said the sophist, in an undertone
Gruff with contempt; which a death-nighing moan
From Lycius answered, as heart-struck and lost,
He sat supine beside the aching ghost.
"Fool! Fool!" repeated he, while his eyes still
Relented not, nor moved; "from every ill
Of life have I preserved thee to this day,
And shall I see thee made a serpent's prey?"

Then Lamia breathed death-breath; the sophist's eye,
Like a sharp spear, went through her utterly,
Keen, cruel, perceant, stinging: she, as well
As her weak hand could any meaning tell,
Motioned him to be silent; vainly so,
He looked and looked again a level - No!
"A Serpent!" echoed he; no sooner said,
Than with a frightful scream she vanished:
And Lycius' arms were empty of delight,
As were his limbs of life, from that same night.
On the high couch he lay! - his friends came round -
Supported him - no pulse, or breath they found,
And, in its marriage robe, the heavy body wound.[35]

As Keats had received some money from various sources whilst in Winchester, including repayment of some loans he had made, he was in a position to purchase some books locally. According to Robert Gittings[36] he used *Titles of*

Honour by John Seldon as background reading for the writing of *King Stephen,* and *Archaeologia Graeca* by John Potter to assist with *Lamia II.* He may well have bought both books in ROBBINS (WELLS) bookshop in College Street, a shop he passed on his daily walk before reaching Winchester College.

Keats's writing was shaped by his imagination, his reaction to immediate experiences, or the use of classical sources to develop a theme with which he was concerned. Background reading was an important factor. He always had with him a copy of Shakespeare's works, he referred greatly to Burton's *The Anatomy of Melancholy* and Milton and Chatterton were in his consciousness, as well as other English writers.

On Monday, 6th September, Brown left him for three weeks. He was now able to devote himself to reading and writing single-mindedly. His money worries had been alleviated temporarily, he had cut himself off from the influence of his friends, and, more importantly, he had temporarily sealed himself off from Fanny. They had not exchanged letters for three weeks. He also enjoyed the excellent weather and felt that his health was certainly improving.

The weather in the autumn of 1819 was particularly fine. Keats comments upon it in his letters thus:

> ....The delightful Weather we have had for two Months is the highest gratification I could receive - no chill'd red noses - no shivering - but fine Atmosphere to think in - a clean towel mark'd with the mangle and a basin of clear Water to drench one's face with ten times a day: no need of much exercise - a Mile a day being quite sufficient - My greatest regret is that I have not been well enough to bathe though I have been two Months by the sea side and live now close to delicious bathing - Still I enjoy the Weather I adore fine Weather as the greatest blessing I can have....[37]

> ....Since I have been at Winchester I have been improving in health - it is not so confined - and there is on one side of the city a dry chalky down where the air is worth six pence a pint. So if you do not get better at Retford do not impute it to your own weakness before you have well considered the nature of the air and soil -

> especially as Autumn is encroaching: for the autumn fogs over a rich land is like the steam from cabbage water.... Our hea[l]th temperament and dispositions are taken more (notwithstanding the contradiction of the history of cain and abel) from the air we breathe than is generally imagined.... Agriculture is the tamer of men; the steam from the earth is like drinking their mother's milk - It enervates their natures...[38]

In this period of physical and psychological wellbeing, between 6th and 10th September 1819, he turned to writing a second version of *Hyperion* - 'The Fall of Hyperion' (the first 180 lines). At the same time he was reading again and preparing for his publisher poems he had written in the past year. Keats's work was interrupted as he had to travel to London on some business. He travelled by the Friday night coach on 10th September. He may well have travelled by the coach advertised in the Hampshire Chronicle and Courtier, the 'Royal

Safety Coach'. It advertised its services as 'a newly invented safety coach which from the peculiarity of its construction precludes the possibility of overturning.' The journey from London to Southampton took nine and a half hours.[39]

Having finished his negotiations in London he wrote the following letter to Fanny Brawne on Monday, 13th September, but he did not go to see her. He felt that he had not yet accomplished his mission to become an acknowledged poet and to have an income from it.

> My dear Girl,
> I have been hurried to Town by a Letter from my brother George; it is not of the brightest intellengenc[e] Am I mad or not? I came by the Friday night coach - and have not yet been to Hamstead. Upon my soul it is not my fault, I cannot resolve to mix any pleasure with my days: they go one like another undistinguishable. If I

were to see you to day it would destroy the half comfortable sullenness I enjoy at present into dow[n]right perplexities. I love you too much to venture to Hampstead, I feel it is not paying a visit, but venturing into a fire. Que feraije? as the french novel writers say in fun, and I in earnest: really what can I do? Knowing well that my life must be passed in fatigue and trouble, I have been endeavouring to wean myself from you: for to myself alone what can be much of a misery? As far as they regard myself I can despise all events: but I cannot cease to love you. This morn[i]ng I scarcely know what I am doing. I am going to Walthamstow - I shall return to Winchester tomorrow; whence you shall hear from me in a few days - I am a Coward, I cannot bear the pain of being happy: t is out of the question: I must admit no thought of it.

Yours ever affectionately,

John Keats[40]

Keats returned to Winchester on Wednesday, 15th September. A day after adjusting to his routine in Winchester, on 17th September, he proceeded to write to George and Georgiana Keats extensively - a letter which, in fact, he continued writing over seven days altogether.[41] In this letter Keats wrote what he referred to as 'a few nonsense verses'[42] for their amusement. As he explained, he was inspired by a story he had read in 'The Spectator' about someone who invited a group of stutterers and squinters to dinner. He was also prompted to think about the effect on a man of being in love, having met someone in such a state recently. Although he would not wish to admit it, he might even have suspected that he gave this impression himself, as his feelings for Fanny might have been very much on his mind. He had, after all, just been to London and had deliberately not seen Fanny, despite perhaps wanting to do so.

In any case, the poem shows Keats's ability to employ irony in his work and is amusing to read:

Pensive they sit, and roll their languid eyes
Nibble their to[a]sts, and cool their tea with sighs,
Or else forget the purpose of the night
Forget their tea - forget their appetite.
See with cross'd arms they sit - ah hapless crew
The fire is going out, and no one rings
For coals, and therefore no coals betty brings.
A Fly is in the milk pot - must he die
Circled by a humane society?
No no there m^{r} Wert[h]er [43]takes his spoon
Inverts it - dips the handle and lo, soon
The little struggler sav'd from perils dark
Across the teaboard draws a long wet mark.
Romeo! Arise! take Snuffers by the handle
There's a large Cauliflower in each candle.
A winding-sheet - Ah me! I must away
To no 7 just beyond the Circus gay.
'Alas' my friend! your Coat sits very well:
Where may your Taylor live'?' 'I may not tell -
'O pardon me - I'm absent now and then"
Where *might* my Taylor live? - I say again
I cannot tell. let me no more be teas'd -
He lives in wapping *might* live where he pleas'd[44]

Pensive they sit and roll their languid eyes ....

After the unsettling experience of going to London, Keats's daily walk was helping him to centre himself again. On 21st September, in a letter to J.H. Reynolds, he comments on the ambience of Winchester:

> ....How beautiful the season is now - How fine the air. A temperate sharpness about it. Really, without joking, chaste weather - Dian skies - I never lik'd stubble fields so much as now - Aye better than the chilly green of the spring. Somehow a stubble plain looks warm - in the same way that some pictures look warm - this struck me so much in my sunday's walk that I composed upon it....[45]

Winchester

The poem he composed on this Sunday, 19th September 1819, was the ode *To Autumn*, inspired by his walk through the Water Meadows. This ode has been the subject of many scholastic interpretations. What distinguishes *To Autumn* is the fact that it is so readily accessible on many levels, to many people. It has the rare quality of a timeless clarity that captures, in the flow of the poet's impressions into words, the very essence of autumn. The immediacy with which Keats wrote this poem, the first stanza of which was barely altered in the original manuscript, conveys the desire that impelled him: to devote himself to 'another sensation'.[46]

The ode *To Autumn* seems to be a pure crystallisation of his poetic state of mind, the reaction to beauty in the autumnal countryside and also perhaps of his subconscious fears about his own 'autumn' - his fear of losing his strength before he had been able to fulfil his ambitions.

To Autumn

Season of mists and mellow fruitfulness,
Close bosom-friend of the maturing sun;
Conspiring with him how to load and bless
With fruit the vines that round the thatch-eaves run;
To bend with apples the moss'd cottage-trees,
And fill all fruit with ripeness to the core;
To swell the gourd, and plump the hazel shells
With a sweet kernel; to set budding more,
And still more, later flowers for the bees,
Until they think warm days will never cease,
For Summer has o'er-brimm'd their clammy cells.

Who hath not seen thee oft amid thy store?
Sometimes whoever seeks abroad may find
Thee sitting careless on a granary floor,
Thy hair soft-lifted by the winnowing wind;
Or on a half-reap'd furrow sound asleep,
Drowsed with the fumes of poppies, while thy hook

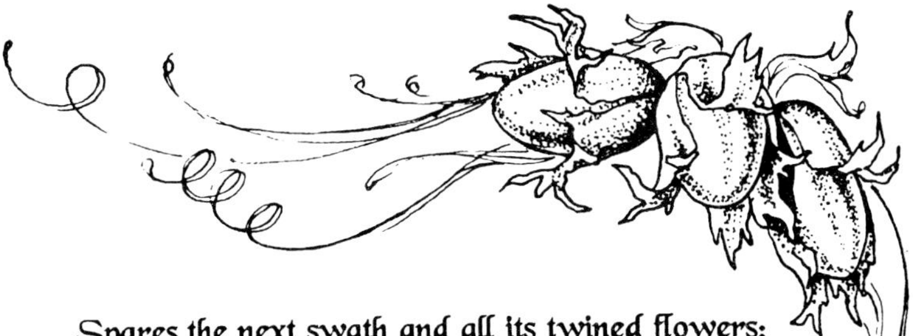

Spares the next swath and all its twined flowers:
And sometimes like a gleaner thou dost keep
Steady thy laden head across a brook;
Or by a cyder-press, with patient look,
Thou watchest the last oozings hours by hours.

Where are the songs of Spring? Ay, where are they?
Think not of them, thou hast thy music too, -
While barred clouds bloom the soft-dying day,
And touch the stubble-plains with rosy hue;
Then in a wailful choir the small gnats mourn
Among the river sallows, borne aloft
Or sinking as the light wind lives or dies;
And full-grown lambs loud bleat from hilly bourn;
Hedge-crickets sing; and now with treble soft
The red-breast whistles from a garden-croft;
And gathering swallows twitter
in the skies.

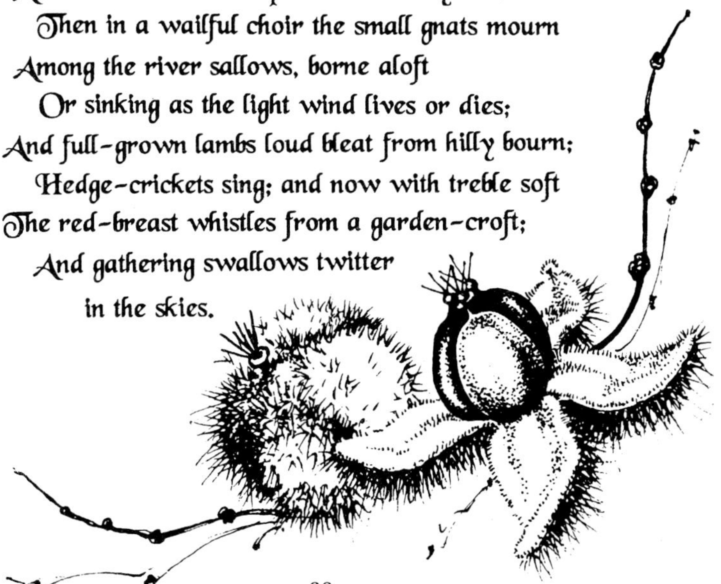

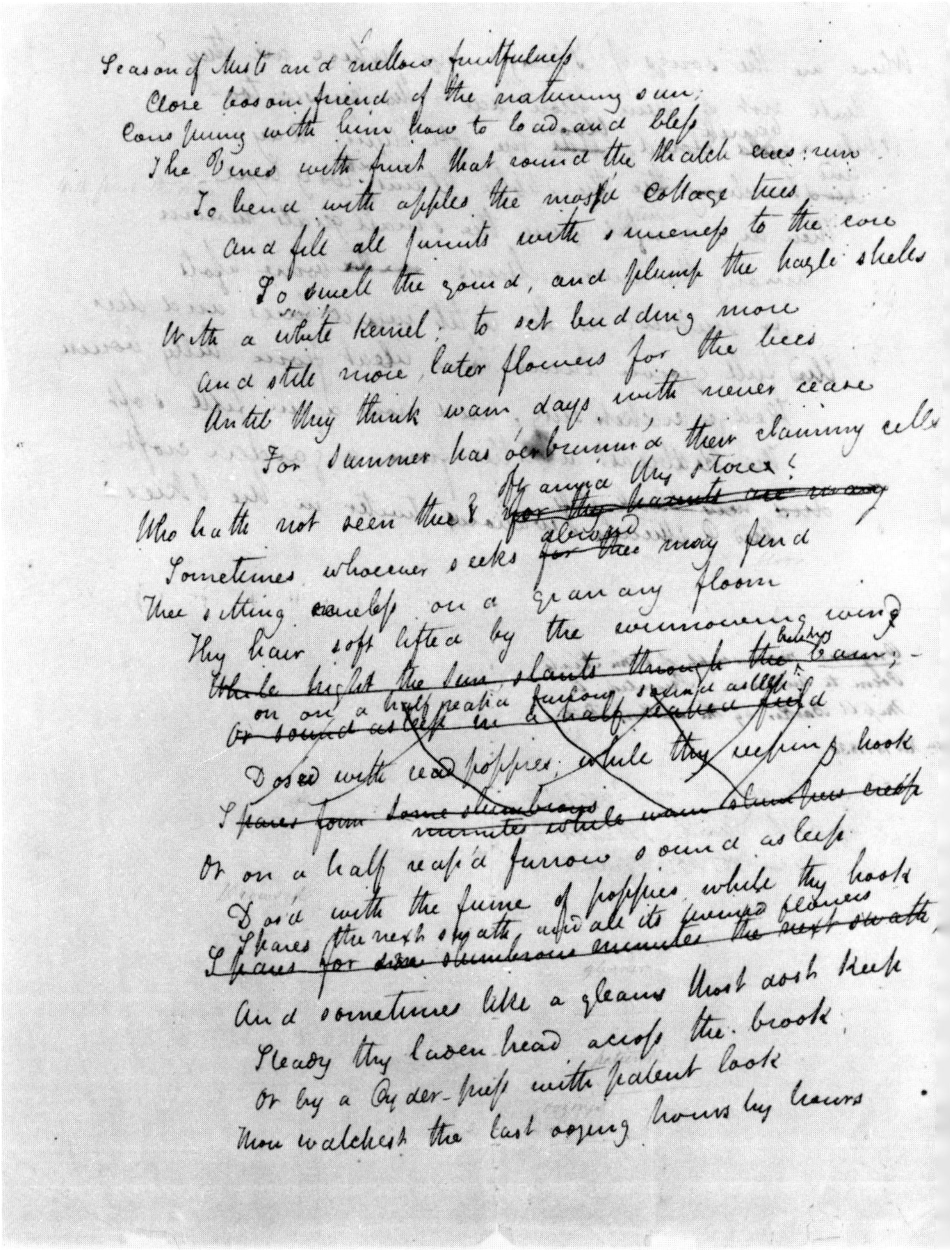
Season of Mists and mellow fruitfulness
Close bosom friend of the maturing sun;
Conspiring with him how to load and bless
The Vines with fruit that round the thatch eves run
To bend with apples the moss'd Cottage trees
And fill all fruits with sweetness to the core
To swell the gourd, and plump the hazle shells
With a white kernel; to set budding more
And still more, later flowers for the bees
Until they think warm days will never cease
For Summer has o'erbrimm'd their clammy cells
Who hath not seen thee? ~~for thy haunts are many~~ [Oft amid thy stores]
Sometimes whoever seeks ~~for thee~~ [abroad] may find
Thee sitting careless on a granary floor
Thy hair soft lifted by the winnowing wind;
~~While bright the Sun slants through the barn;~~
[or on a half reap'd furrow sound asleep]
~~Or sound asleep in a half reaped field~~
Dosed with red poppies; while thy reeping hook
~~Spares form Some slumbrous minutes while warm slumbers creep~~
Or on a half reap'd furrow sound asleep
Dos'd with the fume of poppies, while thy hook
[Spares the next swath and all its twined flowers]
~~Spares for some slumbrous minutes the next swath~~
And sometimes like a gleaner thou dost keep
Steady thy laden head across the brook;
Or by a Cyder-press with patient look
Thou watchest the last oozing hours by hours

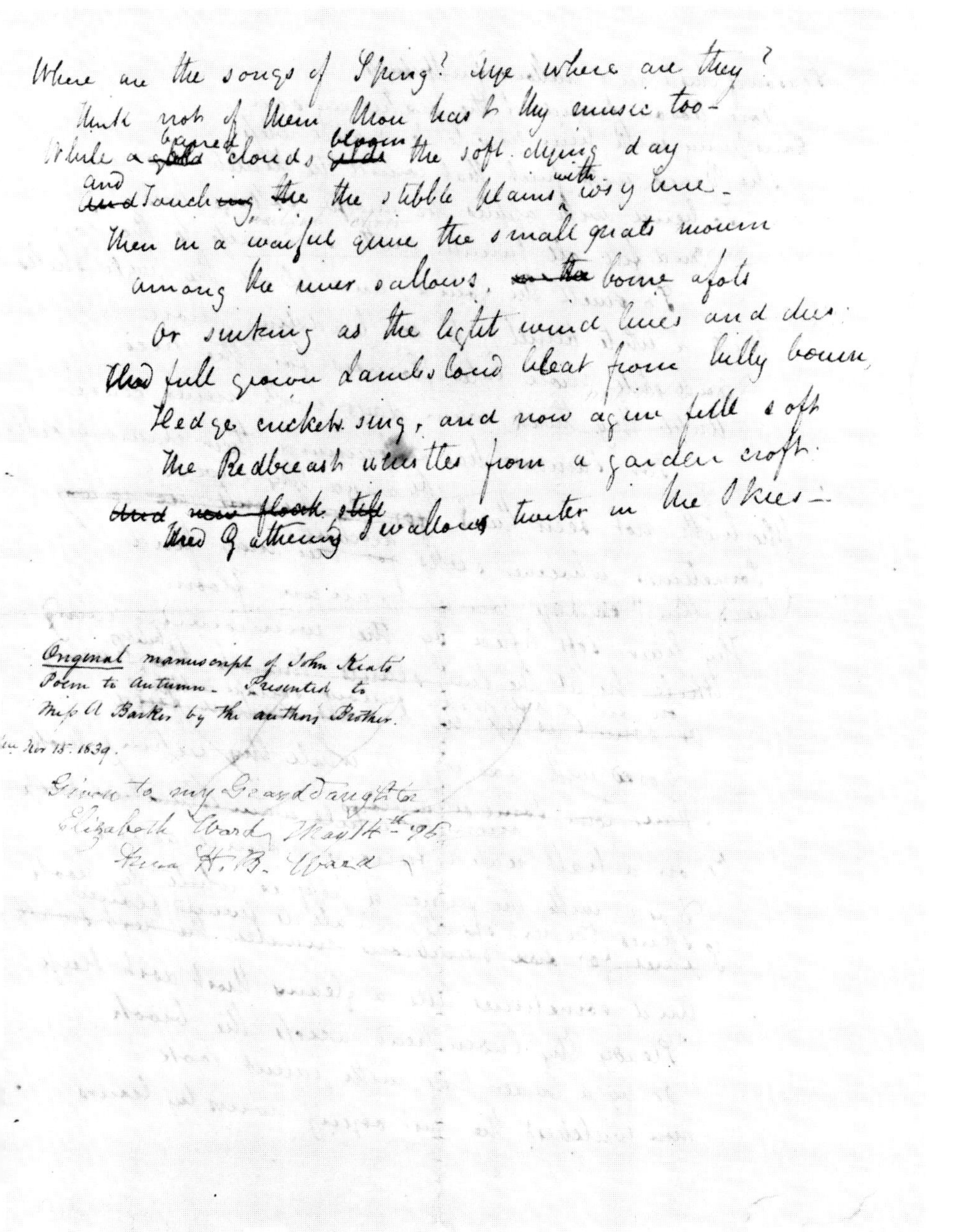

Where are the songs of Spring? Aye where are they?
Think not of them thou hast thy music too—
While a ~~gold~~ [barred] clouds ~~gild~~ [bloom] the soft-dying day
~~And~~ [and] Touch~~ing~~ the the stubble plains [with] rosy hue—
Then in a wailful quire the small gnats mourn
Among the river sallows, ~~on the~~ borne aloft
Or sinking as the light wind lives and dies;
~~And~~ full grown Lambs loud bleat from hilly bourn;
Hedge crickets sing, and now again full soft
The Redbreast whistles from a garden croft:
~~And now flock still~~
Then Gathering Swallows twitter in the Skies—

Original manuscript of John Keats Poem to Autumn – Presented to Miss A Barker by the authors Brother.
Nov 18. 1839.

Given to my Granddaughter
Elizabeth Ward March 14th – 96.
Emma H. B. Ward

Manuscript of ode *To Autumn* by permission of the Houghton Library, Harvard University

The other attempt at writing in this new style, *The Fall of Hyperion*, had not proved so successful. Here, he found the transition from his old way of writing difficult. So much so that in a letter dated 21st September he told J.H. Reynolds:

> ....I have given up Hyperion - there were too many Miltonic inversions in it - Miltonic verse cannot be written but in an artful or rather artist's humour. I wish to give myself up to other sensations. English ought to be kept up. It may be interesting to you to pick out some lines from Hyperion and put a mark × to the false beauty proceeding from art, and one // to the true voice of feeling. Upon my soul 'twas imagination I cannot make the distinction - Every now & then there is a Miltonic intonation - But I cannot make the division properly....[47]

VI

Two recurring themes Keats was contemplating during his solitary existence in Winchester were concerned with his own self and with his attitude to literature. Both topics are reflected in his Winchester letters. Keats's words speak for themselves:

> ....I am surprized myself at the pleasure I live alone in.....
>
> ....To night I am all in a mist; I scarcely know what's what - But you knowing my unsteady & vagarish disposition, will guess that all this turmoil will be settled by tomorrow morning. It strikes me to night that I have led a very odd sort of life for the two or three last years - Here & there - No anchor - I am glad of it.....

....I would give a guinea to be a reasonable man - good sound sense - a says what he thinks, and does what he says man - and did not take snuff - They say men near death however mad they may have been, come to their senses - I hope I shall here in this letter - there is a decent space to be very sensible in - many a good proverb has been in less....[48]

....My occupation is entirely literary; I will do so too. I will write, on the liberal side of the question, for whoever will pay me. I have not known yet what it is to be diligent. I purpose living in town in a cheap lodging, and endeavouring, for a beginning, to get the theatricals of some paper. When I can afford to compose deliberate poems I will....[49]

....I mean I should *do* something for my immediate welfare - ....I would willingly have recourse to other means. I cannot; I am fit for nothing but literature. Wait for the issue of this Tragedy? No - there cannot be greater uncertainties east west, north, and south than concerning dramatic composition. How many months must I wait! Had I not better begin to look about me now?....[50]

....Within these two Months I have written 1500 Lines, most of which besides many more of prior composition you will probably see by next Winter. I have written two Tales, one from Boccacio call'd the Pot of Basil; and another call'd St Agnes' Eve on a popular superstition; and a third call'd Lamia - (half finished - I [hav]e a[l]so been writing parts of my Hyperion and [c]ompleted 4 Acts of a Tragedy. It was the opinion of most of my friends that I should never be able to [write] a [s]cene - I will endeavour to wipe awa[y the prejudice -] I sincerely hope you will be pleased when my Labours since we last saw each other shall reach you - One of my Ambitions is to make as great a revolution in modern dramatic writing as Kean has done in acting - another to upset the drawling of the blue stocking literary world - if in the course of a few years I do these two things I ought to die content - and my friends should drink a dozen of Claret on my Tomb - I am convinced more and more every day that (excepting the human friend Philosopher) a fine writer is the most genuine Being in the World - Shakspeare and the paradise Lost every day become greater wonders to me - *I look upon fine Phrases like a Lover.....*[51]

....I feel every confidence that if I choose I may be a popular writer; that I will never be; but for all that I will get a livelihood - I equally dislike the favour of the public with the love of a woman - they are both a cloying treacle to the wings of independence. I shall ever consider them (People) as debtors to me for verses, not myself to them for admiration - which I can do without. I have of late been indulging my spleen by composing a preface *at* them: after all resolving never to write a preface at all "There are so many verses," would I have said to them", give me so much means to buy pleasure with as a relief to my hours of labour - You will observe at the end of this if you put down the Letter "How a solitarry life engenders pride and egotism!" True: I know it does but this Pride and egotism will enable me to write finer things than any thing else could - so I will indulge it - Just so much as I am hu[m]bled by the genius above my grasp, am I exalted and look with hate and contempt upon the literary world - A Drummer boy who holds out his hand familiarly to a field marshall - that Drummer boy with me is the good word and favour of the public - Who would wish to be among the commonplace crowd of the little-famous - who are each individually lost in a throng made up of themselfes? is this worth louting or playing the hypocrite for? To beg suffrages for a seat on the benches of a myriad aristocracy in Letters?....[52]

....I am convinced more and more day by day that fine writing is next to fine doing the top thing in the world; the Paradise Lost becomes a greater wonder - The more I know what my diligence may in time probably effect; the more does my heart distend with Pride and Obstinacy - I feel it in my power to become a popular writer - I feel it in my strength to refuse the poisonous suffrage of a public - My own being which I know to be becomes of more consequence to me than the crowds of Shadows in the Shape of Man and women that inhabit the kingdom. The Soul is a world of itself and has enough to do in its own home ....

....I could pass my Life very nearly alone though it should last eighty years. But I feel my Body too weak to support me to the height; I am obliged continually to check myself and strive to be nothing. It would be vain for me to endeavour after a more reasonable manner of writing to you: I have nothing to speak of but myself - and what can I say but what I feel? If you should have any reason to regret this state of excitement in me, I will turn the tide of your feelings in the right channel by mentioning that it is the only state for the best sort of Poetry - that is all I care for, all I live for....[53]

....The Paradise lost though so fine in itself is a corruption of our Language - it should be kept as it is unique - a curiosity. a beautiful and grand Curiosity.........The purest english I think - or what ought to be the purest - is Chatterton's - The Language had existed long enough to be entirely uncorrupted of Chaucer's gallicisms and still the old words are used - Chatterton's language is entirely northern - I prefer the native music of it to Milton's cut by feet I have but lately stood on my guard against Milton. Life to him would be death to me. Miltonic verse cannot be written but it [*for* in] the vein of the art - I wish to devote myself to another sensation - ....The only means of strengthening one's intellect is to make up one's mind about nothing - to let the mind be a thoroughfare for all thoughts....[54]

....You speak of Lord Byron and me - There is this great difference between us . He describes what he sees - I describe what I imagine - Mine is the hardest task. You see the immense difference - The Edinburgh review are affraid to touch upom [*for* upon] my Poem - They do not know what to make of it - they do not like to condemn it and they will not p[r]aise it for fear - They are as shy of it as I should be of wearing a Quaker's hat - The fact is they have no real taste - they dare not compromise their Judgements on so puzzling a Question - If on my next Publication they should praise me and so lug in Endymion - I will address [them] in a manner they will not at all relish - The Cowardliness of the Edinburgh is worse than the abuse of the Quarterly....[55]

VII

The weekend around 19th September was a time for decisions. Having had the (presumably) satisfying experience on Sunday of writing a pleasing poem and taking stock of his experiences the previous week, Keats set about writing letters to his friends, making his intentions known. To

Richard Woodhouse he wrote on 21st and 22nd September:

> ....Now I am going to be serious - After revolving certain circumstances in my Mind; chiefly connected with a late american letter - I have determined to take up my abode in a cheap Lodgings in Town and get employment in some of our elegant Periodical Works - I will no longer live upon hopes - I shall carry my plan into execution speedily - I shall live in Westminster - from which a walk to the British Museum will be noisy and muddy - but otherwise pleasant enough - I shall enquire of Hazlitt how the figures of the market stand....[56]

On 22nd September he also wrote to Charles Brown:

> Now I am going to enter on the subject of self. It is quite time I should set myself doing something, and live no longer upon hopes. I have never yet exerted myself. I am getting into an idle minded, vicious way of life, almost content to live upon others. In no period of my life have I acted with any self will, but in

throwing up the apothecary-profession. That I do not repent of'

....If you live at Hampstead next winter - I like xxxxxxxx (omitted by copyist - probably 'Miss Brawne') and I cannot help it. On that account I had better not live there. While I have some immediate cash, I had better settle myself quietly, and fag on as others do. I shall apply to Hazlitt, who knows the market as well as anyone, for something to bring me in a few pounds as soon as possible. I shall not suffer my pride to hinder me. The whisper may go round; I shall not hear it. If I can get an article in the "Edinburg", I will....[57]

And to C. W. Dilke on 22nd September

....I have written to Brown on the subject, and can but go over the same Ground with you in a very short time, it not being more in length than the ordinary paces between the Wickets. It concerns a resolution I have taken to endeavour to acqu[i]re something by temporary writing in periodical works. You must agree with me how unwise it is to keep feeding upon hopes, which depending so much on the state of temper and imagination, appear gloomy or bright, near or afar off just as it happens - Now an act has three parts - to act, to do, and to perform - I mean I should *do* something for my immediate welfare - Even if I am swept away like a Spider from a drawing room I am determined to spin ....Therefore will you look about Marsham, or rodney [*for* Romney] street for a couple of rooms for me....[58]

Again, to Charles Brown on 23rd September, 1918

....Nay, I am convinced, out and out, that by prosing for awhile in periodical works I may maintain myself decently.[59]

Finally, again to C. W. Dilke on 1st October, 1819

For sundry reasons, which I will explain to you when I come to Town, I have to request you will do me a great favor as I must call it knowing how great a Bore it is. That your imagination may not have time to take too great an alarm I state immediatly that I want you to hire me a couple of rooms in Westminster. Quietness and ch[e]apness are the essentials: but as I shall with Brown be returned by next Friday you cannot in that space have sufficient time to make any choice selection, and need not be very particular as I

> can when on the spot suit myself at leisure. Brown bids me remind you not to send the Examiners after the third....[60]

Keats left Winchester on 8th October and moved into lodgings in Great College Street, Westminster. His intention had been to refrain from contacting Fanny Brawne but, on 10th October, he did visit her and immediately came under her spell again. His letter to her, dated 11th October, links up with the love letters he had sent to her from Shanklin, prior to coming to Winchester and cutting himself off from her.

> I am living to day in yesterday: I was in a complete fa[s]cination all day. I feel myself at your mercy. Write me ever so few lines and tell you [*for* me] you will never for ever be less kind to me than yesterday - You dazzled me - There is nothing in the world so bright and delicate - When Brown came out with that seemingly true story again[s]t me last night, I felt it would be death to me if you had ever believed it -

though against any one else I could muster up my obstinacy - Before I knew Brown could disprove it I was for the moment miserable. When shall we pass a day alone? I have had a thousand kisses, for which with my whole soul I thank love - but if you should deny me the thousand and first - 't would put me to the proof how great a misery I could live through. If you should ever carry your threat yesterday into execution - believe me 't is not my pride, my vanity or any petty passion would torment me - really 't would hurt my heart - I could not bear it - I have seen Mrs. Dilke this morning - she says she will come with me any fine day - [61]

This moment I have set myself to copy some verses out fair. I cannot proceed with any degree of content. I must write you a line or two and see if that will assist in dismissing you from my Mind for ever so short a time. Upon my Soul I can think of nothing else - The time is passed when I had power to advise and warn you again[s]t the unpromising morning of my Life - My love has made me selfish. I cannot exist without you - I am forgetful of everything but seeing you again - my Life seems to stop there - I see no further. You have absorb'd me. I have a sensation at the present moment as though I was dissolving - I should

> be exquisitely miserable without the hope of soon seeing you. I should be affraid to separate myself far from you. My sweet Fanny, will your heart never change? My love, will it? I have no limit now to my love - You note came in just here - I cannot be happier away from you -'T is richer than an Argosy of Pearles. Do not threat me even in jest. I have been astonished that Men could die Martyrs for religion - I have shudder'd at it - I shudder no more - I could be martyr'd for my Religion - Love is my religion - I could die for that - I could die for you. My Creed is Love and you are its only tenet - You have ravish'd me away by a power I cannot resist: and yet I could resist till I saw you; and even since I have seen you I have endeavoured often "to reason against the reasons of my Love." I can do that no more - the pain would be too great - My Love is selfish - I cannot breathe without you.[62]

Following this visit, Keats started living with Brown at Wentworth Place again.[63] His health declined steadily. On 3rd February 1820 he had his first haemorrhage. It was becoming increasingly clear that he had contracted pulmonary tuberculosis, possibly having become infected when nursing his brother, Tom. In May, Keats moved to Kentish Town near Leigh Hunt. On 22nd June he had a second severe haemorrhage and moved to Leigh Hunt's house.

In July, 1820 his final volume of poetry, *Lamia, Isabella, The Eve of Saint Agnes and Other Poems,* was published. This collection also contained the ode *To Autumn.* The reviews were positive and thus Keats had at least one set of encouraging reviews during his life-time. However, commercially the collection was not a success.

Keats's health continued to worsen and in August

he left Hunt's house and returned to Wentworth Place, where Mrs. Brawne nursed him. Keats's doctors suggested that the only thing that might help was a stay in Italy over the winter. He left England on 17th September, accompanied by his friend Joseph Severn, the painter. They travelled on the sailing brig 'Maria Crowther'. His publisher and friend John Taylor had raised the money for the voyage and the expenses in Italy. He also arranged for lodgings at 26 Piazza di Spagna, Rome and engaged an English doctor, James Clark. (26 Piazza di Spagna was purchased by the Keats-Shelley Memorial Association and is now the Keats-Shelley Memorial House, open to the public).

Severn cared for Keats devotedly and dealt with all his correspondence. Keats's room was relatively small, with a blue ceiling on which white flowers with golden centres were painted.[64] The murmering water from the fountain in the Piazza below his windows provided a background murmuring to his thoughts. Perhaps it was this that inspired him to request the words 'Here lies one whose name was writ in water' be inscribed on his gravestone. Although Keats had been quite prescriptive about this wording for his gravestone, Brown actually preceded Keats's words with the following: 'This GRAVE contains all that was Mortal of a YOUNG ENGLISH POET Who on his Death Bed, in the Bitterness of his Heart at the Malicious Power of his Enemies Desired these Words to be engraved on his Tomb Stone.'

This inscription later caused controversy among his friends. In a later letter to Severn, Brown expresses his great regret for not obeying Keats's directive:

> ....While I sincerely thank you for referring the subject of a bas-relief and other matters to me, conjointly with yourself, I must decline having anything to do with the monument, - except on one point. This point is that not one word shall be there except those contained in this dying request - "Here lies one whose name was writ in water". Swayed by a very natural feeling at the time, I advised more, but now I am convinced of the error, the sort of profanation of adding even a note of admiration to his own words. If a dying friend, a good man, leaves strict orders for the wording of his epitaph, he should be obeyed, if good faith is in the world. I have long repented of my fault, and must repeat what I said to you in Rome, "I hope the government will permit the erasure of every word, with the exception of those words to which he himself limited his epitaph.[65]

We shall, of course, never know what Keats intended the sentence on his gravestone to mean. There have been many interpretations. Perhaps I may add my own: as Keats had attended lectures by Hazlitt in London on continental poetry, he may well have heard of a poem by the German contemporary poet Johann Wolfgang von Goethe (1749-1832):

Gesang der Geister über den Wassern[66]	Song of the Spirits above the Water
Des Menschen Seele	Man's soul
Gleicht dem Wasser;	Is like the water;
Vom Himmel kommt es,	It comes from Heaven,
Zum Himmel steigt es,	It rises to Heaven,
Und wieder nieder	And down to Earth
Zur Erde muß es,	It must return again,
Ewig wechselnd.	In an eternal cycle.

If Keats was aware of this poem , it puts a different perspective on the sentence by which he wanted to be remembered. Perhaps Keats was reflecting in his choice of epitaph an affirming sense of himself as part of the ever-renewing cycle of life: his soul, as his name, ‘writ in water’; flowing, ebbing, rising and returning.

VIII

Keats had come to Winchester to find a library. He was disappointed on that score. However, it can be argued that instead he found something infinitely more precious: relatively good health, peace of mind and a regular life-style in a town exuding a well-ordered life, with beautiful surroundings which he appreciated. His stay here caused him to take stock of his own life and to decide that he needed to put his life on a viable footing, instead of relying on his friends and hoping to live on the publication of his poems alone. His realistic approach also included the resolve to live in London away from his love, Fanny, because he had come to appreciate how much he needed single-mindedness to be effective in his writing. The history of his life shows, however, that he would not have the strength, after all, to stay away from Hampstead as intended, once he had seen Fanny again.

Most importantly, of course, his regular walk through the Water Meadows inspired one of the finest poems in the English language, *To Autumn,* and the history of one of Winchester's kings, *King Stephen,* led Keats to write the first act of a play which, had he finished it, might well have established his reputation as a playwright.

To have given Keats a period of centred and fulfilled existence must be considered a great satisfaction for Winchester. The Water Meadows have barely changed, and King Stephen's history can be traced to the Great Hall, where his picture can now be seen in a window on the eastern wall. Thus we are able to create a link between what Keats might have felt and seen, and what we perceive today - despite the passage of time since his stay in Winchester.

Notes

[1] *Letters of John Keats*, ed. Robert Gittings, Oxford University, Oxford, 1987, p. 315.
[2] as 1, pp.318-9, to the George Keatses.
[3] now 'Keats House', Wentworth Place, Keats Grove, Hampstead, London, NW3 2RR, which has been open to the public since 9th. May 1925.
[4] At Keats's time and given that his brother Tom had died from tuberculosis, Keats may well have taken this as an early sign of having contracted tuberculosis.
[5] The biographical information contained in this chapter has been taken from *Keats House Hampstead*, text by Christina M. Gee, and permission to publish the material obtained from London Borough of Camden.
[6] Walter S. Scott, *The Poetical Works of John Keats*, James & Co. Ltd., 1902, p. XIII.
[7] Christina M. Gee, *Keats House Hampstead*, London Borough of Camden, 1990, p. 2.
[8] as 1, p. 266, to Fanny Brawne.
[9] as 1, p. 268, to Fanny Brawne.
[10] as 1, p. 270, to Fanny Brawne.
[11] as 1, p. 276, to Fanny Brawne.
[12] as 1, p. 270, to Fanny Brawne.
[13] as 1, p. 276, to Benjamin Bailey.
[14] as 1, p. 278, to Fanny Brawne.
[15] as 1, p. 282, to Fanny Brawne.
[16] as 1, p. 286, to John Taylor.
[17] as 1, pp. 314-5, to the George Keatses.
[18] as 1, pp. 308-9, to the George Keatses.
[19] as 1, p. 333, to B.R. Haydon.
[20] *Hampshire Chronicle and Courtier South and West of England Pilot*, 14th. August to 4th October 1819.
[21] as 1, p. 278, to Fanny Brawne.
[22] as 1, p. 322, to the George Keatses.
[23] This assumption is based on literature of the period.

[24] This street plan was kindly supplied by Mrs. Christina M. Gee, of 'Keats House', Hampstead and it was published in the *Cornhill Magazine* of February 1921.
[25] Barry Shurlock in his *The Winchester Story*, Milestone Publications, 1986 states on p. 75 that the path discernable on the right was called 'Keats Walk'.
[26] see Katherine Kenyon, *Keats in Winchester*, 1947.
[27] Keats means Albrecht Dürer, the German artist.
[28] Charles Ball, *An Historical Account of Winchester with Descriptive Walks*, printed by James Robbins, College St., Winchester, 1818.
[29] I owe this information to the staff of the Winchester Cathedral Education Centre.
[30] Robert Gittings, *John Keats, The Living Year*, Mercury Books, London, 1962, p. 167.
[31]as 30, p. 164.
[32] This information was supplied by a member of staff in 'The Great Hall', Winchester.
[33] as 1, p. 305, to George and Georgina Keats.
[34] as 30, p. 168.
[35] as 6, p. 284.
[36] as 30, p. 196.
[37] as 1, p. 283, to Fanny Brawne.
[38] as 1, pp. 286-7, to John Taylor.
[39] advertisement appearing regularly in the *Hampshire Chronicle and Courtier* of the period.
[40] as 1, p. 290, to Fanny Brawne.
[41] as 1, Letter to George and Georgina Keats, 17, 18, 20, 21, 24, 25, 27 September 1819, p. 304 ff.
[42] as 1, p. 307, to the George Keatses.
[43] Werther was a cult figure resulting from J.W. von Goethe's early novel *Die Leiden des Jungen Werther*, translated by Richard Graves as: *The Sorrows of Young Werther: A German Story*.
[44] as 1, p. 307, to the George Keatses.
[45] as 1, p. 322, to the George Keatses.
[46] as 1, p. 292, to J.H. Reynolds.
[47] as 1, p. 292, to J.H. Reynolds.
[48] as 1, p. 292, to J.H. Reynolds.
[49] as 1, p. 299, to Charles Brown.
[50] as 1, p. 301, to Charles Brown.
[51] as 1, p. 276, to Benjamin Bailey.
[52] as 1, p. 280, to John Taylor.

[53] as 1, pp. 281-2, to J.H. Reynolds.
[54] as 1, pp. 325-6, to the George Keatses.
[55] as 1, p. 314, to the George Keatses.
[56] as 1, p. 297, to Richard Woodhouse.
[57] as 1, p. 299, to Charles Brown.
[58] as 1, p. 301, to C.W. Dilke.
[59] as 1, p. 304, to Charles Brown.
[60] as 1, p. 330, to C.W. Dilke.
[61] as 1, p. 333, to B.R. Haydon.
[62] as 1, p. 334, to Fanny Brawne.
[63] The now following biographical information is taken from Christina M. Gee, *Keats House, Hampstead*, London Borough of Camden, 1990.
[64] Vera Cacciatore, *A Room in Rome*, The Keats-Shelley Memorial Association, Rome, London, New York, 1973, p. 40.
[65] as 64, p. 56.
[66] Emil Staiger, *Johann Wolfgang Goethe*, Insel Verlag, 1977, p. 75.

Bibliography

Vera Cacciatore, *A Room in Rome*, The Keats-Shelley Memorial Association, Rome, London, New York, 1973

Elizabeth Cook (ed.), *John Keats*, Oxford University Press, Oxford, 1994

Christina M. Gee, *Keats House Hampstead*, published by London Borough of Camden, 1990

Robert Gittings, *John Keats, The Living Year*, Mercury Books, London, 1962

Robert Gittings, (a selection edited by) *Letters of John Keats*, Oxford Uiversity Press, 1987

Katherine M.R. Kenyon, *Keats in Winchester*, Warren & Son Ltd., 1947

Walter S. Scott, *The Poetical Works of John Keats*, James Finch and Co. Ltd., London, 1902

Barry Shurlock, *The Winchester Story*, Milestone Publications, 1986

The John Keats Memorial Volume, issued by The Keats House Committee, Hampstead, John Lane, The Bodley Head, London, 1921

Winchester Illustrated, ed. by William Thorne Warren, Warren & Son Ltd., 1913